E
jHUT   Hutchins, Pat.

1 hunter.

$16.95   Preschool
                04-0927

DATE			

1 hunter

by PAT HUTCHINS

Greenwillow Books, New York

For Harry—Number One

1 Hunter
Copyright © 1982 by Pat Hutchins
All rights reserved. Printed in Hong Kong
by Printing Express Ltd.
www.harperchildrens.com
First Edition
15 14 13 12

Library of Congress
Cataloging-in-Publication Data
Hutchins, Pat (date)   1 hunter.
"Greenwillow Books."
Summary: One hunter walks through the
forest observed first by two elephants,
then by three giraffes, etc.
1. Counting—Juvenile literature.
[1. Counting. 2. Animals—Fiction.]
I. Title.
QA113.H87   513'.2 [E]   81-6352
ISBN 0-688-00614-0   AACR2
ISBN 0-688-00615-9 (lib. bdg.)
ISBN 0-688-06522-8 (pbk.)

1 hunter

 elephants

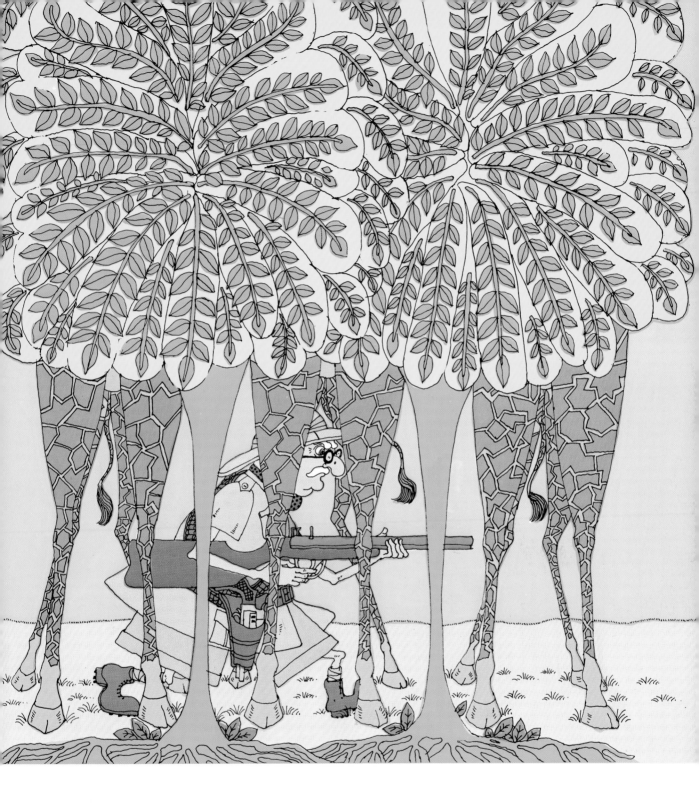

3 giraffes

4 ostriches

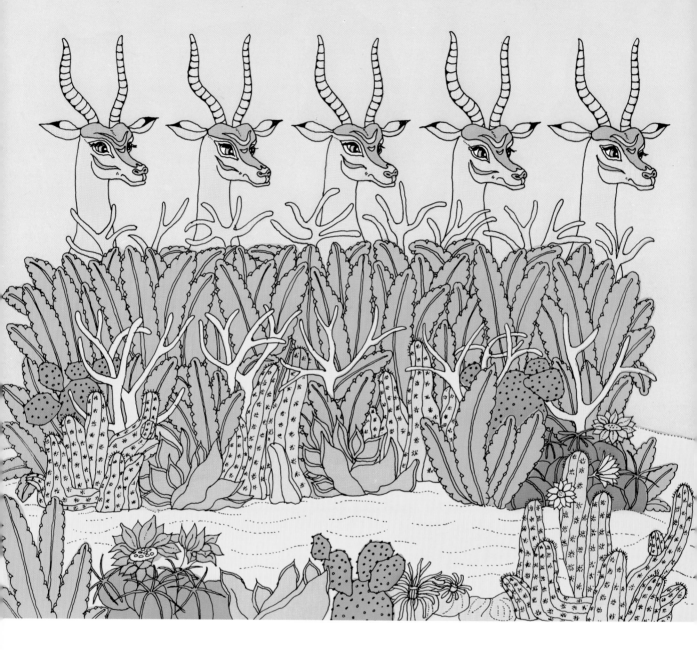

5 antelopes

6 tigers

7 crocodiles

8 monkeys

 snakes

10 parrots

10 parrots **9** snakes **8** monkeys

7 crocodiles **6** tigers **5** antelopes

4 ostriches   3 giraffes   2 elephants

and 1 hunter